Bacon Saturday Mornings

by Cassia McClain
illustrated by Deborah White

Richard C. Owen Publishers, Inc.
Katonah, New York

On Saturday mornings, my momma cooks
hash browns and pancakes and bacon and eggs
for breakfast. Mmmmmmm! I love
the smell of bacon.

Momma stands by the stove wearing
her special Saturday morning dress.
Her hair looks soft and shiny when the
sun comes in through the cracks of the
kitchen blinds. She looks so pretty.

"What would you like for breakfast?"
Momma asks me.

"I know I want bacon," I tell Momma.
"And eggs, too, but mostly bacon."

I *love* bacon.

3

"I guess you can have all that," she says.

"Just remember there are six others in this house who haven't eaten yet. So leave some for them, all right?" she says, smiling at me.

"Yes Momma," I say.

She hands me my plate.
Mmmmm! Breakfast is so good
on Saturdays, better than any other day.

Now, what should I do today?
I wonder as I sit in the kitchen with Momma.

Oh, I know. I could go outside and skateboard
or play on my swing or . . .

I could walk barefoot on the hot sidewalk,
then dash into the cool grass or . . .

I could ask Momma if I could turn on the sprinkler
and sit on top of it or . . .

I could hunt for frogs or . . .

I could go for a ride with my dad.
He'd turn on music, take me all over town,
and tell me funny stories and jokes.

If I call up my friend Kelly, she could come over
and jump rope with me. I could do
that, or . . .

I could go to my room, listen to my favorite CD,
take out my pad and pencil, and write a story.
The words would all come alive inside my mind.

I could draw pictures for my story and sign it
World's Greatest Writer
and tape it up on the wall
over my sister's bed.

But then I look up and see Momma, Momma wearing her special Saturday morning dress, looking so pretty, humming and singing her favorite song.
Everything is so warm and happy in the kitchen. I want to stay here with Momma.

I join in and sing with Momma.

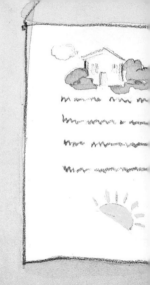

I *love* being with Momma
on bacon Saturday mornings.